ELMER AND THE LOST TEDDY

David McKee

Andersen Press
London

The sky was already dark and full of stars when Elmer,
the patchwork elephant, heard the sound of crying.
It was Baby Elephant.
   "He can't sleep," said Baby Elephant's mother.
"He wants his teddy. We took Teddy with us on a picnic
and somewhere we lost it."

"Never mind," said Elmer. "I'll lend him my teddy.
Tomorrow I'll look for the lost one."
    Elmer went away and came back with his teddy.
Baby Elephant smiled and was soon fast asleep
with Elmer's teddy beside him.

The next day Elmer set off in search of the lost teddy.
He hadn't gone far when he met his cousin, Wilbur.

"Hello, Wilbur," said Elmer. "I'm looking for Baby Elephant's
lost teddy. Have you seen it?"

"No," said Wilbur. "But if I find it, I'll call you."

A little later a voice said, "Hello, Elmer. Where are you going?" It was Lion.

"Baby Elephant has lost his teddy and I'm looking for it," said Elmer.

"Oh dear," said Lion. "Baby Lion would be very upset if he lost his teddy. If I find it, I'll call you. Maybe Tiger has seen it."

As he came near Tiger's place, Elmer called out, "Yoho! Tiger!"
"Ssssh! Elmer," Tiger quietly called back. "The twins are asleep."
"Sorry," said Elmer. "Only, Baby Elephant has lost his teddy.
Have you seen it?"
"That's serious," said Tiger. "The twins wouldn't sleep
without their teddies. If I find it, I'll call you."

After that, Elmer visited the other animals.
All the young ones had their teddies, but none of them
had seen Baby Elephant's. They all said the same thing,
"If we find it, we'll call you."

It was getting late into the afternoon and Teddy was still lost.
"I hope I find him soon," thought Elmer. "It's nearly night time."
It was at that moment that he heard a shout. "Help! Help!"
And then again: "Help! I'm lost!"

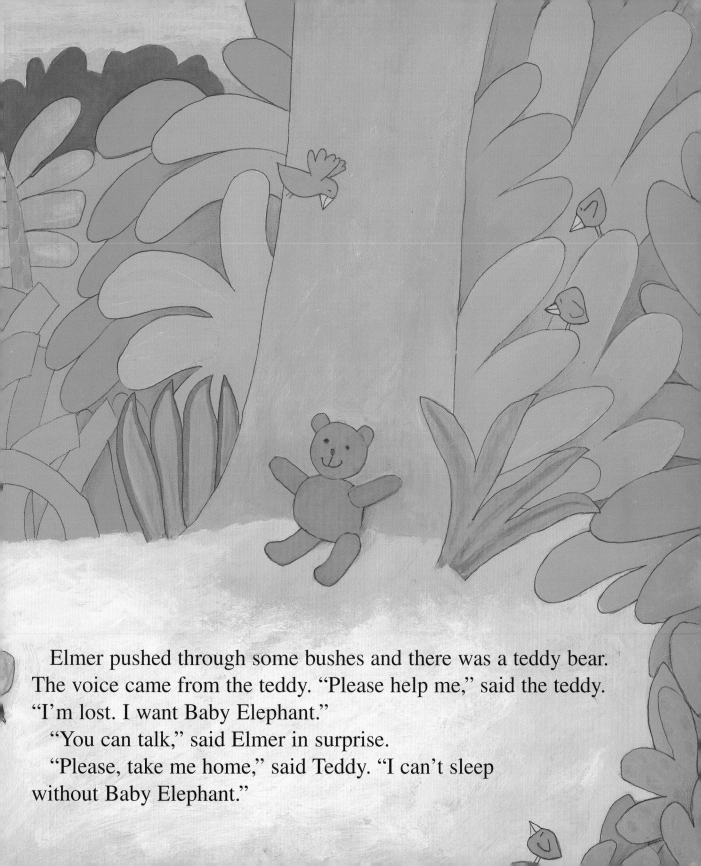

Elmer pushed through some bushes and there was a teddy bear. The voice came from the teddy. "Please help me," said the teddy. "I'm lost. I want Baby Elephant."

"You can talk," said Elmer in surprise.

"Please, take me home," said Teddy. "I can't sleep without Baby Elephant."

Elmer still stared. "Your mouth isn't moving," he said.
Just then Wilbur appeared from the bushes.

"Wilbur," laughed Elmer. "I might have known it was you making Teddy speak."

Wilbur chuckled. "I said I'd call you if I found Teddy," he said. "And I did. Come on, let's take Teddy home, it's getting dark."

They set off together, singing as they went.

Baby Elephant was excited to see his teddy again
and quickly gave back Elmer's teddy.

Baby Elephant's mother couldn't thank Elmer and Wilbur enough.

"Elmer," said Wilbur, "weren't you worried that Baby Elephant would want to keep your teddy? Your teddy is very different; it's special."

"But, Wilbur, didn't you know?" said Elmer in surprise.
"You don't have to be different to be special. All teddies are
special, especially your own."